AF174074

# Do You Feel Anger?

*by* Mara Nelson-Greenberg

SAMUELFRENCH.COM    SAMUELFRENCH.CO.UK

## FOR PRODUCTION ENQUIRIES

UNITED STATES AND CANADA
Info@SamuelFrench.com
1-866-598-8449

UNITED KINGDOM AND EUROPE
Plays@SamuelFrench.co.uk
020-7255-4302

Each title is subject to availability from Samuel French, depending upon country of performance. Please be aware that *DO YOU FEEL ANGER?* may not be licensed by Samuel French in your territory. Professional and amateur producers should contact the nearest Samuel French office or licensing partner to verify availability.

## MUSIC USE NOTE

Licensees are solely responsible for obtaining formal written permission from copyright owners to use copyrighted music in the performance of this play and are strongly cautioned to do so. If no such permission is obtained by the licensee, then the licensee must use only original music that the licensee owns and controls. Licensees are solely responsible and liable for all music clearances and shall indemnify the copyright owners of the play(s) and their licensing agent, Samuel French, against any costs, expenses, losses and liabilities arising from the use of music by licensees. Please contact the appropriate music licensing authority in your territory for the rights to any incidental music.

## IMPORTANT BILLING AND CREDIT REQUIREMENTS

If you have obtained performance rights to this title, please refer to your licensing agreement for important billing and credit requirements.

*DO YOU FEEL ANGER?* received its world premiere in the 42nd Humana Festival of New American Plays at the Actors Theatre of Louisville in Louisville, Kentucky on March 9, 2018. New York on March 13, 2019. The performance was directed by Margot Bordelon, with sets by Arnulfo Maldonado, costumes by Jessica Pabst, lights by Isabella Byrd, sound by M.L. Dogg, and dramaturgy by Jenni Page-White. The production stage manager was Katie Shade. The cast was as follows:

| | |
|---|---|
| **SOFIA** | Tiffany Villarin |
| **EVA** | Megan Hill |
| **JON** | Dennis William Grimes |
| **HOWIE** | Amir Wachterman |
| **JORDAN** | Bjorn DuPaty |
| **SOFIA'S MOTHER / JANIE** | Lisa Tejero |
| **OLD MAN** | Jon Huffman |

*DO YOU FEEL ANGER?* was produced by the Vineyard Theatre, Douglas Aibel, Artistic Director, Sarah Stern, Artistic Director, Suzanne Appel, Managing Director, in New York, New York on March 13, 2019. The performance was directed by Margot Bordelon, with sets by Laura Jellinek, costumes by Emilio Sosa, lights by Marie Yokoyama, original music and sound design by Palmer Hefferan, and wig, hair, and makeup design by J. Jared Janas. The production stage manager was Adrian White. The cast was as follows:

| | |
|---|---|
| **SOFIA** | Tiffany Villarin |
| **EVA** | Megan Hill |
| **JON** | Greg Keller |
| **HOWIE** | Justin Long |
| **JORDAN** | Ugo Chukwu |
| **SOFIA'S MOTHER / JANIE** | Jeanne Sakata |
| **OLD MAN** | Tom Aulino |

# CHARACTERS

**SOFIA** – late 20s

**EVA** – early 30s

**JON** – late 40s

**HOWIE** – early 30s

**JORDAN** – late 20s

**SOFIA'S MOTHER** – mid-50s

**JANIE** – any age (may be doubled with **SOFIA'S MOTHER**)

**OLD MAN** – 130

# PRE-RECORDED

**DONNA** – 60s

**MAN'S VOICE** – any age

# SETTING

Most of the stage is a conference room with glass walls. It is attached to a phone bank just offstage, and people cross behind the room every so often.

In the conference room there is one chair that stays empty the whole time. A cardigan hangs over the back of the chair, and a cup of coffee sits on the table in front of it.

Towards the very end of the play, bathroom stalls appear onstage.

# CASTING NOTES

Howie should be played by a white actor. Between Jordan and Jon at least one of the roles should be played by a person of color, and between Eva and Sofia at least one of the roles should be played by a person of color.

More generally, this is a play about power, violence, and complicity. With that in mind re: your casting decisions, please be mindful of not perpetuating insidious stereotypes, and please be aware of what story you are telling based on the actors you cast in each role.

# PERFORMANCE NOTES

The actors should play against the menace rather than leaning into it, especially at the top of the play. For example, when Howie says he'd like to have sex with Sofia, it should sound more like he'd like to grab a coffee with her than being an aggressive come-on.

*For my mother.*

## Scene One

(**SOFIA'S MOTHER** *is leaving* **SOFIA** *a voice message.*)

**SOFIA'S MOTHER.** Hi, dear. Just checking in. I know you're starting your new assignment today, and you must be very busy, but... I just wanted to say hi and wish you luck! Not that you *need* my luck... I realize that I'm talking to the person who once taught a broker without tear ducts how to cry out of his *mouth*...

(*Pause.*)

Anyways – I hope you're okay. I haven't heard from you since – well, since your father wrote you, so... I just wanted to see how you're doing.

(*Pause.*)

And let's see...what else. Oh! Sherry told me about this beautiful island called Compass Point, with these gorgeous views, and sea creatures that talk to you and keep you company as you swim. And so...maybe we can go together after your job!

(*Pause.*)

I know you must be processing some...*complicated* feelings right now, so... I just wanted to let you know that... I'm here if you want to talk. I love you my little spider. Okay – bye bye.

(**SOFIA** *is in the conference room, setting up a tape recorder and some papers.* **EVA** *enters.*)

**EVA.** Hi! I'm Eva.

**SOFIA.** Hi, Eva. I'm Sofia.

**EVA.** You're here to try and help us scream less at people on the phone?

**SOFIA.** Yes. I'm an empathy coach.

**EVA.** To be honest, I don't think I need lessons on empathy. But everyone else in the office does, so.

>   *(She laughs.)*

You're going to love it here. I know you hear "debt collection agency," and you think everyone in this office must be really mean, but you're right. It's a very small, insular community here, and everyone *is so* outgoing and mean and it's just a really fantastic, really scary work environment. Someone keeps mugging me when I'm walking around the office.

>   *(She smiles.)*

I like your nails – are they from your hands?

**SOFIA.** Did you say someone keeps mugging you?

**EVA.** I don't think so! Did you say that?

**SOFIA.** *You* said that.

**EVA.** If you say so. Someone keeps mugging me, so it wouldn't be so crazy for me to say it out loud, but I'd certainly never dwell on it or claim that's what's happening. Someone keeps mugging me.

>   *(Pause.)*

You seem lovely. Everyone here's going to hit on you.

**SOFIA.** Oh, well...thank you.

**EVA.** I'm trying to say that like it's a compliment, but really it's a warning. Everyone's going to hit on you, and you won't get anything done unless you shut it down. And even if you *do* shut it down, eventually they'll find a way around it and then they'll wear you down until you disappear.

**SOFIA.** Well, if people hit on me, I'll just tell them to stop.

**EVA.** What do you mean?

**SOFIA.** I'll say, "Please don't hit on me."

**EVA.** *(Laughing.)* No!

>   *(More frantic.)*

**EVA.** No, no – no. That doesn't seem like the best way to handle it. Maybe you should...are you dating anyone?

**SOFIA.** No, I'm not. Can I ask why that's relevant?

**EVA.** Okay, well...

(*Pause.*)

Maybe you want to *start* dating someone like, ASAP? I *just* broke up with my boyfriend – I was with him for ten years, even though I hated him the whole time. His name was – Marcus? Marco? Hold on – I could never pay attention to him when he was talking, so... I wrote it down. Okay...his name was...

(*Checking a piece of paper.*)

Jeffrey.

(*Pause.*)

Weird. Where did I get Marcus from?

(*Pause.*)

Anyways, Marcus – sorry, *blagh* – *Jeffrey* was a marine biologist, which sounds interesting, but it was *really* not...

(*Taking out a photo.*)

This is a photo from a trip we took upstate with a few friends...he's...

(*Looking at the photo.*)

Which one *is* he?

(*Looking.*)

Oh – there he is. There, or there. One of those two guys was my Marcus. Shoot! My *Jeffrey*. It's so weird that I keep doing that. I don't even *know* any Marcuses, besides my dad.

**SOFIA.** Why did you guys break up?

**EVA.** Well – first, he started cheating on me – mostly getting hundreds of blowjobs from other women – and then eventually he ended up *murdering*...

**SOFIA.** He ended up *murdering*?

**EVA.** Or, no – what's it called when you stab someone to death?

**SOFIA.** Murder.

**EVA.** Okay, so then yeah – he ended up murdering! And even then, I didn't really want to break up with him, because he was *so* helpful for the work dynamics, but I was like – he murdered more than one person, so...you know the saying.

**SOFIA.** I'm not sure I do.

**EVA.** No?

> *(As if it's a rhyme.)*

"If he murders one / It's all in good fun. / If he slaughters a whole crowd, and you realize you were sharing a bed with a stranger for ten years just to avoid a bad work environment..."

> *(She pauses.)*

Huh. *What* is the ending to that saying? "Just to avoid a bad work environment...something something something and serial killers' wives always finish last."

**SOFIA.** Well – good for you, that you got out of an unhealthy relationship.

**EVA.** Thanks, yeah, it's made my life so stressful, because now I'm scrambling to get a new boyfriend ASAP so that my work-life can return to normal. Like – this date I went on last night?

> *(She shakes her head.)*

I mean, he wasn't terrible, but he said the phrase, "Egg is a man's best egg," a lot so, you know, just...not the perfect fit.

**SOFIA.** Can we go back to what you said before? About how someone's mugging you?

**EVA.** What? Oh no, that's okay, but thanks.

> *(She smiles.)*

**EVA.** Maybe we can just recap my advice instead: try to date someone like my dad Marcus – sorry, my *boyfriend*, Marcus – sorry, *my ex-boyfriend* Jeffrey, and then mention that person all the time, but do it really subtly, and then never break up with him, even if he turns out to be a murderer, or – sorry – a "stabber to death."

*(She laughs.)*

Because I wouldn't want you to end up in danger.

**SOFIA.** Danger how?

**EVA.** Like me – like how I'm in danger. And, I mean... I know that they keep saying Janie's just in the bathroom, but...it's been so many days!

*(She laughs. **SOFIA** doesn't know why, but she laughs too. **JON** enters.)*

**JON.** Eva? Could I have a second with Sofia alone?

**EVA.** Of course!

*(Playfully nodding to **JON** and **SOFIA**.)*

M'lady. M'sir.

*(She giggles and then exits.)*

**JON.** So! All set for today?

**SOFIA.** Ah – yes! I was planning on checking out some of those calls, and then – can I just ask – Eva said something about being mugged in the office?

**JON.** Do you mean Janie?

**SOFIA.** I think – wasn't that Eva just now?

**JON.** Oh, Eva! Yes. She's spoken to me about that and I'm over it. Sorry – *all* over it. The safety of my employees is my *top* priority. Bottom line, over everything else, I really want to pretend that I'm a "good guy."

*(He laughs, then pauses thoughtfully.)*

Isn't the situation with the homeless terrible? Just awful. They don't have much food but they have to eat to survive.

**SOFIA.** Right.

*(She smiles.)*

**SOFIA.** And so did they explain how this works? Basically, I take your employees through the training, and once it's clear they understand the material, I sign the form they sent you, we pass it back up to head office, and we're done!

**JON.** Okay – so I imagine it won't take more than a day or two.

**SOFIA.** It usually takes closer to four or five weeks.

**JON.** Well, maybe in *other* offices. I know that you're used to intense clients – your office told me about the doctors you helped, who had forgotten that humans weren't objects – but I think you'll actually find that, so long as you quickly ingratiate yourself into the environment here, this is a fantastic place to work. For example – we have maternity leave now, where we let women leave when they're giving birth. To be honest, head office insisted on this, but I'm not even sure we *need* empathy lessons in the first place.

**SOFIA.** Except that – I see that you had another incident *just* last night. One of your employees was on the phone with someone and made up a new curse word and used it upwards of – forty-seven –

**JON.** *(Overlapping.)* Forty-seven times, yes. Although to be fair, it *was* an accurate description of what he wanted to do to her.

**SOFIA.** I think some empathy training could help you avoid a situation like that altogether. I'm going to turn this office into an empathy engine!

**JON.** *(Nodding, thinking.)* Okay...

*(Pause.)*

And what *is* empathy, exactly? Is that...a type of...it's not a bird.

**SOFIA.** No, it's...empathy is the ability to understand other people's feelings.

**JON.** Like – hunger. And anger.

**SOFIA.** And sadness, or elation, or fear...

**JON.** And hunger, or anger – or horn.

**SOFIA.** Horn?

**JON.** When you want to have sex with someone.

**SOFIA.** Sure. The beauty about our feelings is that they're complicated, and they're hard to pin down, and each and every one of them is valid. And I'm excited to unpack it all with you.

(*Off his look.*)

Look, Jon – I can see you're a little skeptical –

**JON.** Oh no! It's not that I have anything against *you* personally. I'm just protective over my employees! We've been together a long time, you know, and we're more than an office at this point – we're like a little family.

(*He pauses and smiles.*)

Warts and all! Unresolved anger and all! Love and familial abuse and decades of bubbling resentment and ongoing power struggles and all!

**SOFIA.** Well – I'm not here to *mess* with your...family. I want to strengthen it.

**JON.** Yeah, sure. I've heard *that* before.

(*Explaining.*)

I come from a pretty *dysfunctional* family myself.

**SOFIA.** I know *all about it.*

(*He looks a little doubtful.*)

Really, Jon – I can relate.

(*He shakes his head with shame.*)

**JON.** No, but I'm talking like – imagine...*a divorce.*

(*Pause.*)

That's what it was – my parents got divorced. You could never understand.

**SOFIA.** (*She decides on something.*) You know what? Empathy in action!

(*Pause.*)

SOFIA. I do understand your feelings around a dysfunctional family, Jon, because – well, *just this week*, in fact, I found out my father has...a second family.

(*Pause.*)

Which he told me in an e-mail.

JON. He told you...in an *e-mail*?

SOFIA. To be fair, he's always been a little – you know – *thoughtless*, but –

JON. Can I see it?

SOFIA. No!

JON. Right. I'm sorry I asked. That was inappropriate.

(*Pause.*)

It's just that – I'm supposed to write my niece and explain why I'm not invited to Thanksgiving dinner anymore. But it's been kind of hard to...

(*He trails off as he pulls up an e-mail and shows it to* SOFIA.)

SOFIA. (*Reading.*) "Dear Becca, Happy ninth birthday. I have something to tell you."

(*Pause.*)

"Justice Potter Stewart once said about hard-core pornography, 'I know it when I see it.'"

(*She continues reading to herself, then stops.*)

What's a Piss Chart?

JON. It's what I love. But see? I get stuck towards the end. And I want to get it right.

(*Pause.*)

Just because I don't only love Piss Charts, you know. I *also* love my niece.

(SOFIA *studies* JON.)

SOFIA. Well – fine, Jon. If you want to take a look at his e-mail...it's not perfect, but it's self-reflective, so...

(**SOFIA** *shows* **JON** *an e-mail and he begins to read it.*)

**JON.** "Dear Sofia, I'm sorry that you had to find out that I have a second family this way, in this letter, right now, sort of slipped in here as the direct object of this sentence. I'll be the first to admit that I messed up, but honestly, at some point your mother completely stopped meeting me halfway, and that was really hurtful. I only hope that *you'll* meet me halfway with all of this because, not to get too vulnerable on you, but that's what I want. And if you don't, I'll run off and get a second daughter! Just kidding, I already have one, but that doesn't mean that I don't love you with all my heart. Big hug, my little spider. I'm in pain. Love, Daddy." Sofia – do you have a lot of rage? Towards your father?

**SOFIA.** No – *no*! I feel really sad for him.

**JON.** Even with this PS that he added here?

**SOFIA.** Oh – the –

**JON.** "PS – I also wandered away from your mother because she didn't like giving blowjobs without my ever reciprocating, and I love blowjobs without reciprocation. Oh, I'm sorry – there's no *way* I would have talked about how much I love blowjobs without reciprocation I love blowjobs without reciprocation I love blowjobs without reciprocation. What was I saying? I meant there's no way I would have talked about how much I love blowjobs without reciprocation – I *do* love blowjobs without reciprocation. I really love them a lot. Okay – see you later."

**SOFIA.** I think he just doesn't always know how to practice empathy, because no one ever *taught* him. Which I think is kind of heartbreaking! And it's funny, because –

**JON.** Oh – yes, it is! I love jokes! Well, it's good you're not angry, because this place really doesn't allow anger, except for in very specific circumstances.

**JON**. And also –

>(*He smiles and studies her.*)

Hm.

**SOFIA**. What?

**JON**. Well – I want to say this delicately, so –
(*In a soft British accent.*) You may excel more at your job if you wear a dress.

**SOFIA**. Did you just tell me to wear a dress?

**JON**. No. At least not in my normal voice!

**SOFIA**. I tend to be most comfortable in pants.

**JON**. Great then dress wear a dress.

**SOFIA**. Well, thanks for the tip. I appreciate this whole welcome.

**JON**. Don't mention it.

>(*He studies her.*)

You know, you're not half bad. Although – that's also what they said about my cousin Ralph, until they found out what he does inside his shed, so...

>(*Handing her some tapes.*)

But anyway, here are the tapes. Feel free to go over them, and then you can meet everyone later today!

>(*He exits.*)

### Scene Two

(**SOFIA** *is sitting in the conference room, waiting for the meeting to start.* **JORDAN** *and* **HOWIE** *enter together.*)

**HOWIE.** You're in Janie's chair.

**SOFIA.** Oh – I'll move. There's mold growing in her coffee.

(*She stands up.* **JON** *enters as* **JORDAN** *extends his hand to her.*)

**JORDAN.** I'm Jordan. It's a pleasure for you to meet me. Au chawnj-jay.

**JON.** Jordan – what did we learn about you recently, after you spoke with that client in Paris?

**JORDAN.** We learned I can't speak French.

(*Pause.*)

We also learned that the way I was saying "medium rare steak," it actually meant, "big dog no friends." So yes, I'm Jordan. And *bu la du ma la plont*, but only on weeknights, okay?

(*He laughs.*)

Au chawnj-jay.

**HOWIE.** I'm Howie. I have a terrible temper.

**SOFIA.** Hi, Howie.

(*To* **JON.**) I thought...didn't you say terrible tempers weren't allowed here?

**JON.** Well – like I said – only in particular circumstances, like if you're Howie.

(**EVA** *enters.*)

**SOFIA.** Eva – do *you* have a terrible temper?

**EVA.** What? No! Why? Did someone say I did?

**SOFIA.** No.

**EVA.** Good – because I don't. Instead of anger, I choose to feel – what's the word for "nothing"?

**SOFIA.** Nothing.

**EVA**. Well, I feel whatever the word would be for "nothing," if it existed.

(*She sits down in a chair.*)

Whew! I had an excellent first date last night. Or as my new boyfriend would say, an *egg*-celent first date.

**JORDAN**. What?

**HOWIE**. Who is he?

**EVA**. Well, his full name is actually Michaelangelo, but he just goes by Ra-*fal*-gore.

(*Pause.*)

It was good, yeah. Sort of. Not perfect. He's mean and his hands are always sticky and he calls sugar "sweet pellets" and he has a floating kneecap that he talks about like it's a friend.

(*Pause.*)

But at least I won't end up like Janie – single and getting punched in the face and in the bathroom for an eternity.

**HOWIE**. Well...you're not like *Janie*. Janie was crazy.

**SOFIA**. Janie was crazy?

**EVA**. Big time.

**JORDAN**. Yeah. I mean, I know that there's sort of a taboo against calling women crazy these days – and rightly so, because hargahla *mon*da bonder, but she was definitely a little...*batty*.

**HOWIE**. A *little batty*? We're talking about someone who once threatened to light the whole *office* on fire.

**SOFIA**. What? Why?

**EVA**. I have *no* idea. She just – snapped.

**HOWIE**. Yeah. One minute she was fine, and the next she was wielding this pack of matches like – how familiar are you with Dutch horror films?

**JON**. Janie was a little...challenging. Let's just leave it there.

**HOWIE**. Bitches be crazy!

**JON.** Howie.

**JORDAN.** I think you mean bitches be *batty*.

**JON.** Thank you, Jordan.

**SOFIA.** *(Turning to EVA.)* And – Eva? Before we begin? I was hoping –

**EVA.** Yes – I'm sorry.

**SOFIA.** What are you sorry about?

**EVA.** I didn't...wear...

> *(She looks down.)*

Shoes?

**SOFIA.** You didn't?

> *(Pointing to EVA's feet.)*

Aren't those shoes, though?

**EVA.** Oh, sure. I meant I didn't...go to the...store?

**SOFIA.** You're not in trouble. I was just hoping to talk to you privately after the meeting.

**EVA.** Oh – sure.

**HOWIE.** Excuse me, "with all due respect" in quotes, why are you here? I could be making calls right now.

**SOFIA.** Well – my name is Sofia, and –

**JON.** Sofia? Pardon the interruption, but maybe you'd like to introduce yourself to the group?

**SOFIA.** Ah – yes. My name is Sofia, and I'm here to do some empathy exercises with all of you.

**HOWIE.** I don't mean to make you feel uncomfortable, but I'd love to have sex with you.

**SOFIA.** That actually does make me feel uncomfortable.

**HOWIE.** Well, I don't mean it to, so.

**SOFIA.** Well, it does.

**HOWIE.** *Okay*...now you've made *me* feel uncomfortable that you said I made you feel uncomfortable. I was just trying to tell you how I feel.

**SOFIA.** And I'm just trying to tell you how *I* feel.

**JORDAN**. If I can make this whole exchange more subtle for a second, I think what Howie *meant* is – the question, "are you dating anyone."

**SOFIA**. Ah. No, I'm not – but please don't hit on me.

**JORDAN**. *What?*

**HOWIE**. *Excuse* me?

*(The men fall silent.)*

**EVA**. Oh, you know what?

*(Everyone turns to look at her.)*

I ate my sister in the uterus.

*(Pause.)*

**JON**. Do you mean absorbed, Eva?

**EVA**. Oh – no, yeah, they use that word, "absorbed," for when one fetus absorbs the other, but no, I ate her. I ripped into her with my hands while my parents watched on the ultrasound machine, screaming, trying to stop me.

*(Pause.)*

**JON**. Okay – well, great! I'll leave you to it, Sofia. And guys – be good, alright?

*(He bows.)*

*Aw chawnj-jay.*

*(He exits. **SOFIA** turns to the employees.)*

**SOFIA**. So – empathy.

*(She writes "Empathy" on the board.)*

First off, what does "Empathy" *mean*?

*(**HOWIE** raises his hand.)*

Howie.

**HOWIE**. When you're angry at someone.

**SOFIA**. I think you're describing anger. But I can...

*(She writes down "Anger." **JORDAN** raises his hand.)*

**JORDAN.** Empathy is a bird.

**SOFIA.** Empathy is the ability to *understand* someone else's feelings.

> *(She writes this down. She continues to jot down notes on the board throughout the rest of the meeting.)*

**HOWIE.** Our job is to collect money from people. There's no time for feelings.

**SOFIA.** Actually, Howie! I understand why you'd think that, but what's so exciting about empathy is that it actually *increases* productivity! People are more cooperative when they feel like they're being heard.

> *(Pause.)*

And I believe that one of the reasons for all of the lawsuits against this office is that people here are neglecting their *listening* skills.

**EVA.** Well – that and all of the threats of physical violence.

**SOFIA.** Yes. Thanks, Eva. So today I want to work on *compassionate listening*, which is a big part of empathy.

**JORDAN.** I don't have any problems with listening.

**SOFIA.** What did I just say, then?

**JORDAN.** You talked about how we're in this – room, you know, with walls, and there's a chair, and – well, people say I'm a poet, which, you know, whatever, I *have* been known to –

> *(He breaks into poet voice.)*

"A *cow* a *man* a *boy* a *light*! A *song* a *rock* a *fish* a *star* –"

**SOFIA.** *(Overlapping.)* Jordan? Jordan?

**JORDAN.** Not right now.

**SOFIA.** How about this? I'm going to play a quick piece of a phone conversation from an employee here – and I won't identify who it is...

> *(She presses play.)*

**HOWIE.** *(On recording.)* Hello, is this Donna Jacobs, from 16 Hampshire?

*(To* **SOFIA.***)* That's me!

**WOMAN'S VOICE.** *(On recording.)* Yes – this is Donna.

**HOWIE.** *(On recording.)* Donna, I am a debt collector with Cash Flow Accounts, CFA, and under federal law I must advise you that this is an attempt to collect a debt and any information given will be used for that purpose. We have a claim in our office from Wharton Industries in the amount of seven hundred and forty-four dollars and forty-eight cents. How are you today?

**DONNA.** *(On recording.)* Well, I'm not too good.

**HOWIE.** *(On recording.)* Um. Fine.

**DONNA.** *(On recording.)* My husband is very sick.

**HOWIE.** Oh, okay. I remember this one.

*(On recording.)* I said that's *fine.*

**DONNA.** *(On recording.)* And I take my debts really seriously, but he's in the hospital again, and...look, *please* – I spoke to someone at Wharton about this on *Monday.* Have you talked to them since Monday?

**HOWIE.** *(On recording.)* Well, shit. I wasn't asking for your whole life's story, bitch.

(**SOFIA** *pauses the recording.*)

You haven't gotten to the bad part yet.

**SOFIA.** Let's just talk about this part of the interaction for now. Does anyone see a problem right off the bat?

**JORDAN.** You're not wearing a dress.

**HOWIE.** Oh yeah.

**SOFIA.** I meant with the phone call.

**EVA.** He said, "Shit, I wasn't asking for your whole life's story, bitch."

**SOFIA.** Great. And why would that be a problem?

(**EVA** *looks at* **HOWIE,** *who glares at her. No one responds.*)

I want to try something. Inside your packets, you'll find a worksheet. I want everyone to think about what

Donna Jacobs just told us, and fill out two or three things that she may be *feeling*. I'll do it too.

*(She writes, then waits.)*

Okay? Everyone finished? Jordan – what do you think Donna may be feeling right now?

*(**JORDAN** looks over at **EVA**'s paper.)*

**JORDAN.** Scared and a shaved.

**SOFIA.** Scared and – a shaved?

**JORDAN.** Scared and –

*(Looking over at **EVA**'s paper and trying to understand the second word.)*

Scared and...a-scorned? Or, what? No – *scarred* and *ashawned*.

**SOFIA.** Are you looking at Eva's paper?

**JORDAN.** No.

**SOFIA.** Eva, what did you write down?

**EVA.** I said, "scared and ashamed."

**HOWIE.** Ashamed isn't a word.

**SOFIA.** Yes it is.

**JORDAN.** Okay, so that's what I wrote down.

**HOWIE.** Same with me. Scared and *ashawmed*. Next!

**SOFIA.** So – let's stay on these adjectives for just a second.

*(She writes on the board: scared and ashamed.)*

Why might Donna be – let's start with scared.

*(**HOWIE** raises his hand.)*

**HOWIE.** Horn.

**SOFIA.** Horn. Oh – horny. You think this woman's horny?

**HOWIE.** What? No, *I'm* horny.

**JORDAN.** That's funny – I'm *also* horny, but I *just* had lunch.

**SOFIA.** So I don't want to talk about what *we're* feeling. I want to talk about what Donna Jacobs is feeling.

**HOWIE**. How are we supposed to do that? We don't know her.

**SOFIA**. Just based on what she said on the phone.

**HOWIE**. I don't understand why someone else's feelings should outweigh mine.

**SOFIA**. Well – they shouldn't *outweigh* yours, but they can be *in conversation* with yours.

**HOWIE**. But that's just giving me extra work.

(*He hits the table, annoyed.*)

I'm *so* hunger right now!

**SOFIA**. Well – Howie. Whether you realized it or not, you've actually just expressed a *feeling* to me, and I appreciate it. We're already on our way!

(*She looks at her sheet, and then writes on the board.*)

I wrote "worried," which is similar to "scared," and then...

(*She writes on the board.*)

*Guilty.* Now – I think this is interesting. Why might she feel *guilty*?

**JORDAN**. If she murdered.

**SOFIA**. Specific to this situation.

**HOWIE**. Because she got into a lot of debt. But that's not *our* fault – she should have thought about that before she spent money that she didn't have.

**SOFIA**. So – thanks for bringing that up, Howie. I think that's really common. "She *should* have." I think we "should" others as a defense mechanism. We say what someone "should" have done to convince ourselves that we would *never* be in their position. But when we do that, we're also ignoring all of the specific things that complicate a person's life! Empathy asks you to *hold* your judgment, and accept...

(*As **SOFIA**'s talking, **HOWIE** has passed a paper to **JORDAN**. They're both laughing.*)

Accept...guys – what's funny?

**HOWIE**. It's about Eva.

> (**HOWIE** *shows the joke to* **EVA**. *She looks, horrified. Pause. She scream-laughs.* **SOFIA** *approaches the men.*)

**SOFIA**. Can I see it, please?

> (**HOWIE** *hands her the picture.*)

I don't understand what I'm looking at here. Who's this on the bottom?

**EVA**. That's Janie, right before she took out the pack of matches. And that's me next to her.

**SOFIA**. *(To* **HOWIE** *and* **JORDAN**.*)* But why are Eva's legs bent up like that?

**HOWIE**. In order to make the joke *funny* – do you not understand jokes?

**SOFIA**. Got it.

> (*Handing the diagram back to* **HOWIE**.*)*

Okay – new rule! Jokes about Eva are not allowed here.

**JORDAN**. But –

**SOFIA**. End of story.

**HOWIE**. You're a bummer, you know that? Why am I even listening to you? I don't *know* you.

> (*He stands up and begins to walk around.*)

**SOFIA**. Howie – please sit down.

**HOWIE**. *(Amused.)* Well, actually – *here*, in this office, I stand whenever I want.

**JORDAN**. And I say *this* poem whenever I want: "Life is an oblong."

**SOFIA**. Well, I'm running this meeting, so I would really appreciate it if we could all abide by *my* rules for now.

**HOWIE**. *Excuse me?*

**EVA**. You know what? I ate my other twin in the mitosis stage –

**SOFIA**. That's all right, Eva.

> (*She turns to* **HOWIE**.*)*

**SOFIA.** I understand that my presence here may be disorienting. But I'm here to help, and I know what I'm doing. So I'm going to ask that you let me run these meetings the way I want to run them.

> *(Pause.)*

Now that being said, Howie expressed that he was hungry, and I want to honor that, so – let's take a break.

**HOWIE.** *(Standing up.)* Yes. I think we *should* take a break.

**JORDAN.** I could eat. I'm super horn right now.

**HOWIE.** Same. Eva –

**SOFIA.** *(Gently to* EVA.*)* Eva –

**JORDAN.** Eva –

**HOWIE.** Eva – do you want to get lunch with me? In a sort of threatening way?

**EVA.** Oh – I'm eating with Rafalgore today.

> *(Thinking.)*

Oh, darn. I bet he'll want eggs.

**SOFIA.** Actually, remember, Eva, I'd like for you to stay behind. And then – maybe *we* can eat together.

**EVA.** *(Relieved.)* Oh – great. Sofia and I are going to eat together.

**HOWIE.** Noice!

> **(HOWIE** *exits.* **JORDAN** *begins to exit, but then hangs back for a second.)*

**JORDAN.** Hey, before I go, I just wanted to say that I'm really glad you're here, and I've totally got your back in private. Okay – see you later!

> *(He exits.)*

**EVA.** Are we – do you actually eat lunch, or...?

**SOFIA.** Yes – I do! But first...

> *(She guides* EVA *to a chair.)*

**EVA.** It's so cool that you're an empathy coach. How did you get into that job?

SOFIA. Oh, actually – my mom found out about it and really encouraged me to apply. Ever since I was little she made me feel like I had this special ability to communicate with – all different kinds of people.

EVA. That's great, that your mother knows you so well. Sometimes, by accident, *my* mother calls me Ear-va.

SOFIA. Well – I'd love to hear more about that. For now – I was listening to *your* calls too, as I was combing through the others. And...

(SOFIA *presses play on a recording.*)

EVA. *(On recording.)* Hello! I am a debt collector with Cash Flow Accounts, CFA, and under federal law I must advise you that this is an attempt to collect a debt and any information given will be used for that purpose. We have a claim in our office from Rye Tech, Inc., in the amount of forty-three dollars and sixty-eight cents. *(To* SOFIA.*)* Seems like that's all...by the book...

(SOFIA *fast-forwards a bit.*)

*(On recording.)* I feel like tigers only do that when they're provoked...

(SOFIA *fast-forwards more.*)

No, no, but I'm *stronger* on the flute...

(SOFIA *fast-forwards more.*)

*(Hysterical laughter.)*

(SOFIA *fast-forwards more.*)

Someone with a mask keeps coming up to me at work and mugging me, usually in the kitchen, and it makes me afraid to eat my lunch. And I'm usually too scared and ashamed to eat breakfast or dinner either.

MAN'S VOICE. *(On recording.)* I said that I'm *willing* to pay the money –

(SOFIA *stops the recording.*)

EVA. Okay, so – shorter conversations?

**SOFIA.** Well, yes. This call lasted for four hours and thirty-two minutes. But I'm more focused on...

*(She presses play again.)*

**EVA.** *(On recording.)* Sometimes, when it's happening, I try to shut my brain off. I pretend I'm someone who no one would ever want to mug – like sometimes I pretend I'm a mermaid...

**MAN'S VOICE.** *(On recording.)* Do you not *want* me to pay? Or is this some kind of a –

*(**SOFIA** stops the recording.)*

**EVA.** I know I broke the rule.

**SOFIA.** What rule?

**EVA.** *(Guessing.)* Don't...talk...about...mermaids? ...

*(Pause.)*

During...times...when...

*(Pauses and sighs; she can't get it.)*

You go to the...*store*...and you...

**SOFIA.** You didn't break a rule. I want to help you with these muggings.

**EVA.** Oh! Thanks, but it's fine. I already sent everyone an e-mail about it, a few months ago.

*(She pulls it up on her phone.)*

"Hi, all! So, so, *so* sorry to bother everyone and I know this is really silly, but I just wanted to drop a quick line to say that someone with a mask keeps mugging me in the kitchen and I would *love* it if they could stop." And then I put five pages of exclamation points so that no one would think I was mad at them.

**SOFIA.** But – with all due respect, the e-mail didn't seem to work.

**EVA.** No, but Howie responded saying, "tooth" period, so I know he got it, which is great.

**SOFIA.** I want to help you.

**EVA.** Thanks, but – it's fine. I'm dating Rafalgore now, which will help. And we'll eat sweet pellets together and try to keep Mr. Knee Cap in place and that will be that.

**SOFIA.** Look. I know it feels *safer* to align yourself with Rafalgore. But if you start expressing yourself honestly, in this office – I promise you that I will have your back. Ditch Rafalgore, and stick with me!

**EVA.** I'll think about it.

**SOFIA.** That's all I ask! Now let's go to lunch.

## Scene Three

(**SOFIA** *is setting up some papers in the conference room. She checks her voice messages.*)

**SOFIA'S MOTHER.** Hi, my little spider. It's been a whole week. It's a little...*unusual* for me not to hear from you for this long. And I thought I'd try you, since – your father said that you called him yesterday, when you were on a lunch break? And...well, so, you must have heard from him that I kicked him out. And it's been good for me, because...more room in all the drawers!

(*Pause.*)

He told me that – people at work are being a little difficult? Do you remember when you were ten, and you went up to our neighbor Timothy, who was such a *grump,* and within minutes you had him talking about his insecurities, and his family –

(*She laughs, then pauses.*)

Just – those difficult people at work are lucky to have you.

(*Pause.*)

And – okay, look. I *know* that your father told you about all of the lawyer-stuff. And you don't need any of the gory details, but I just wanted to say that I really didn't *want* to bring in lawyers. Okay? I just – I felt I had to, and that's all you need to know.

(*Trying to change the subject.*)

And I'm trying to get serious about that trip to Compass Point – but there are so many travel sites! Do you know which one you're supposed to use?

(*Pause.*)

Anyways – call me back. I *love* you my little spider. Bye bye.

(**JON** *enters and she closes her phone.*)

**JON.** Hey, Sofia!

**SOFIA.** Hi Jon! Ah – before I forget – there's no place to dispose of tampons in the women's room?

**JON.** Okay. And is that a riddle?

**SOFIA.** What do you mean?

**JON.** Is tampon a feeling? Or...the doctor's a woman or something?

**SOFIA.** No – tampons. For periods.

**JON.** Okay. And is *that* a riddle?

**SOFIA.** Is...ah...have you ever heard of periods before?

**JON.** You know what? Let me just call up this assistant from head office, and she can just –

(*He picks up the phone.*)

Missy? It's Jon. From the...

(*He looks to* **SOFIA** *and speaks more quietly.*)

From the night with all the hoses.

(*Pause.*)

Okay. Well...

(*Pause.*)

You know what, I'm going to politely abruptly interrupt you right now because I have a question for you. Would you mind looking up what periods are?

(*Pause.*)

That's great. Thanks so much.

(*He hangs up the phone.*)

I forgot I did that to her. But she's going to look into it!

(*He smiles.*)

In the meantime – how are things going?

**SOFIA.** Well – not great. Eva told me yesterday that she's still being mugged. She said someone keeps coming up to her and hitting her across the head?

**JON.** I know, yeah. I decided we should launch a formal investigation into the whole thing.

**SOFIA.** You did? That's – great.

**JON.** What about how *your* work's coming along? Are you ready to sign that form yet?

**SOFIA.** Am I...? No. It's only been a week.

**JON.** Right, but I already told head office that I'd get this taken care of in record time.

**SOFIA.** Well, you might want to let them know that things are actually moving kind of slowly. Yesterday instead of answering any of my questions, *both* Howie and Jordan just kept responding to me by saying they wanted to "set this burn on fire" ...

**JON.** *(Laughing.)* Those guys, yeah. They're a pain in my neck, and Jordan's photography makes me really nauseous, but I love them to death.

> *(Pause.)*

Has Howie said "Baby says No" yet?

**SOFIA.** Ah – no...

**JON.** Well, that's good. Because once that's happened, there's basically no getting through to him. It's three steps: he'll hit the wall, he'll go to sleep, and then...how familiar are you with Dutch horror films?

**SOFIA.** We just need a little more time.

**JON.** You have to be *strategic* about your approach. So do you want some strategy? From someone who knows this place pretty well, and has seen how you talk to my employees?

**SOFIA.** I'm not sure I need *strategy*...

**JON.** We're always using strategy with other people to *some* extent. Think about – well, say – your father. You use strategy with him, right?

**SOFIA.** I wouldn't call it *strategy*... I just – listen to him.

**JON.** Perfect, yeah. The only tip I have for you is simple: Lighten up! Families have customs, quirks – certain ways of doing things. Meanwhile, you're the new stepmom, just entering the home for the first time. And instead of...*ingratiating* yourself with the family, *you're* going – "New rules! Shoes *off* in the house. You're not allowed to hit on me." No one likes that kind of stepmom! I *hated* when *my* stepmom said those things to me.

*(Pause.)*

What *I'd* do, if I were you, is let these guys keep *some* of their customs. They'll be much more open to learning new ones that way. Like how I eventually let my stepmom teach me about forks. And I think you'll actually find that –

*(The phone rings.)*

Sorry – one second.

*(He picks up the phone.)*

Hello? Ah! Missy!

*(He listens.)*

Okay, wonderful. So – periods. What the heck are they?

*(Listens, still chipper.)*

Yeah...

*(Listens, still chipper.)*

Okay...

*(Listens, getting slightly more wary.)*

Okay... Missy – let me stop you. This...doesn't sound right. What's your source?

*(Listens.)*

Personal experience. Well...

*(Listens.)*

And WebMD. So...keep going, then...

*(Listens – more worried.)*

*Okay*...keep going...

*(Listens – more worried.)*

**JON**. Ok*ay*, and then what?

>*(His face turns into panic.)*

And then – *what*?

>*(He listens.)*

Oh my God! No.

>*(He listens.)*

*No, no, no!* Please! No!

>*(He begins to cry.)*

Are you freaking *kidding* me right now. This is the worst day *ever*.

>*(Still sobbing.)*

I want to kill myself. I wish I were dead. I wish I were dead.

>*(He screams into the phone.)*

Just *tell me you made the whole thing up*, Missy!

>*(He listens, gets angry.)*

I don't *care* if you weren't lying, just – *tell me you were* –

>*(He listens.)*

Okay, fine, I'll give you back your chairs, and your dining room table, just...*say that you were lying*!

>*(He listens – gaining control of himself.)*

Yeah?

>*(He listens, starting to smile a little.)*

Really? Are you sure?

>*(He laughs a little.)*

Okay, yeah.
Okay. Okay.

>*(He's laughing and laughing now.)*

All right, Missy – I appreciate it. Thanks for looking into that for me.

*(He hangs up the phone.)*

**JON.** Okay, so now I know! Getting your period means extra pee.

**SOFIA.** ...Extra...pee.

**JON.** *(He sees the others approaching.)* So – I'll leave you to it. And don't forget – customs, customs, customs! Because as I always say, in my classic, thoughtful way...

*(He thinks long and hard.)*

"The wilderness? Oh boy, Mama. That's a big one."

*(He bops her on the nose with his finger.)*

Boop!

*(He exits as EVA enters. SOFIA's phone rings. She silences it.)*

**SOFIA.** Hi, Eva.

**EVA.** Hey! Sorry! Am I interrupting?

**SOFIA.** Oh, no, it's just – my mom.

**EVA.** You can get it.

**SOFIA.** No, it's okay. She's just...

*(She puts the phone away.)*

She's in a tough spot. But –

*(Pause.)*

You know when you look at someone and you're just like, "Man. *Everything* you're doing, I'd do the opposite."

*(She shakes her head.)*

Sorry. Overshare!

**EVA.** Don't worry! I used to overshare all the time because my ovaries were so big they had to manually enlarge my pelvic cavity, but I don't anymore.

**SOFIA.** Did you want to tell me something?

**EVA.** Oh, yes! I did what you said. I broke up with Rafalgore last night!

**SOFIA.** Great! How did it go?

**EVA**. It went well, at first, because he was asleep. Although when he woke up he started describing this awful thing that he likes to do with towels, but – anyways. It's a big weight off.

**SOFIA**. Well, that's great.

> (**JORDAN** *and* **HOWIE** *enter.*)

Hey guys.

> (*They barely nod at her. They're busy looking at a drawing and laughing.*)

What's so funny?

**HOWIE**. It's nothing.

**SOFIA**. Okay, well – how's everyone doing today? Ready to learn about visual communication?

**JORDAN**. I want to set this –

**SOFIA**. Burn on fire, I know, Jordan. But maybe today you'll change your mind – because this exercise is usually pretty fun.

> (*She smiles.*)

So I'm going to show everyone some pictures, and I want us all to name the feelings that are either visibly displayed, or *invisible but implied*, using this list of positive and negative feelings. Let's start off nice and easy.

> (*She holds up a picture of two women laughing.*)

What do you think is happening here?

> (**JORDAN** *and* **HOWIE** *begin laughing again.*)

Okay, guys, seriously – *what* is so funny?

**EVA**. It's about me.

**SOFIA**. But I already said – jokes about Eva –

**HOWIE**. It's not *just* about Eva, though.

**JORDAN**. It's also about you, Sofia, and other women, and a lot of other nouns.

**HOWIE**. And plus, it's a *joke*. Lighten up.

**SOFIA.** Can *I* see it?

> (**JORDAN** *hands her the picture.*)

Are those...our appendixes?

> (*Handing the diagram back to the men.*)

No. I don't like this.

**HOWIE.** Wow.

**JORDAN.** Okay.

**HOWIE.** Eva? Do you *also* hate our funny joke?

**EVA.** I...ah... I'm going to go to the bathroom, really quickly.

> (**EVA** *exits.*)

**HOWIE.** Do women sync up when they go to the bathroom?

**SOFIA.** Oh, well –

**HOWIE.** Jordan? Do women sync up when they go to the bathroom?

**JORDAN.** The thing they've realized, after doing lots of research, is that no one knows what syncing up actually *is*. Also, everyone's starting to say that the clitoris is a hoax.

**HOWIE.** I thought syncing up was when they all got a little extra pee at the same time. Or maybe it just means this...

> (*He points to the diagram again and he and* **JORDAN** *start laughing.*)

Wait, no – we can't laugh about that, remember? Feelings only matter in this room when they come from people who have grossly mismanaged their finances.

**SOFIA.** Howie? Put the diagram away, please.

> (*He puts the picture away, frustrated.*)

Thanks.

**HOWIE.** Bad Mommy.

**SOFIA.** Okay. Let's keep going with this exercise, and Eva can jump in when she's back. So take a look at that list of feelings...

*(She starts handing out sheets.* **HOWIE** *is angry as he takes a sheet and she clocks it.)*

**SOFIA.** If you guys want to take a look...

**HOWIE.** *(Looking at the list.)* These aren't even real words. *Norvis?*

**SOFIA.** You mean – nervous?

**HOWIE.** No – I mean that I feel *angry* that I am being told what I can and cannot think is funny.

**SOFIA.** Howie – please. I'm not asking you to change your whole *worldview* here.

**HOWIE.** Baby says No.

*(***HOWIE*** *falls asleep.)*

**JORDAN.** Uh oh. Sound the alarm.

**SOFIA.** Wait!

*(Pause.)*

Wait for just – wait for *just* a second.

Howie? Howie! I understand why you're *angry*, because I've just – swooped in here, and...

*(Pause.)*

You know what? I think I just didn't *understand* the joke.

*(***JORDAN*** *looks at her skeptically.)*

I'm serious. Can I see it again?

*(***HOWIE*** *wakes up to hand her the diagram.)*

Okay, so – I see the catfish, and there's Janie in the corner, with blood on her nose, and Eva is calling her crazy, and all of the other women are –

*(Realizing.)*

Oh. *This* is a Piss Chart.

*(She looks at it, disgusted.)*

I get it. That's really funny.

*(She scream-laughs.)*

**HOWIE**. You like the joke?

**SOFIA**. I like the joke.

**HOWIE**. *(Approaching her.)* That's very cool of you.

**SOFIA**. Also! I have a boyfriend. I have a boyfriend, Marcus.

**JORDAN**. Oh, no.

**HOWIE**. Oh *no*.

**JORDAN**. I *never* meant to disrespect Marcus.

**HOWIE**. Where does he work?

**SOFIA**. He works at... Jeffrey and...

> *(She looks down at her shoes.)*

Shoes.

**HOWIE**. Oh – sure! I know him. Right? Jordan?

**JORDAN**. Of course! Marcus from Jeffrey and Shoes!

**HOWIE**. We were all on a team together, ages ago. Does he still eat lunch?

**SOFIA**. Yeah – he still eats lunch.

**JORDAN**. Is he still obsessed with ponds?

**SOFIA**. Is he still...yeah. He is.

**JORDAN**. *(Laughing like: Classic Marcus!)* Yeah. He's such a good guy.

**SOFIA**. Yeah, I'll tell him you say hi.

**HOWIE**. Great.

**SOFIA**. In the meantime...how would you feel about getting back into this exercise?

**HOWIE**. For Marcus's lover? Baby says *yes*. So...

> *(He looks at the picture.)*

Well – when I look at this picture, I feel – that word you taught us before. Horn.

**SOFIA**. So I want to focus on what *these women* are feeling.

**JORDAN**. Maybe they're...

> *(Looking at the picture.)*

When you don't feel safe.

**SOFIA**. Scared.

**JORDAN.** Right. These women are scared.

**SOFIA.** These women are – scared?

**JORDAN.** They have their danger-faces on.

**HOWIE.** Oh, duh! Which means one of them...has a gun? Or – a guy off to the *side* has a gun.

**JORDAN.** Is that what's invisible but implied?

**HOWIE.** Maybe there's a chainsaw event offstage?

**SOFIA.** But think about a scared person. Right?

*(She makes a scared face.)*

**HOWIE.** Oh, you look like my aunt, after I showed her how I brush my teeth.

**SOFIA.** How about – maybe you guys can think back to a time when *you* were laughing.

**HOWIE.** When we were – oh! Maybe these women just saw a Piss Chart.

**JORDAN.** So they're – happy?

*(Excited pause.)*

**SOFIA.** Yes, Jordan! These women are happy! Good – that's great! And so now –

*(**EVA** enters.)*

**EVA.** Guys? I have something to say.

*(She takes a deep breath.)*

I think that picture you showed us before...is *not* funny.

**JORDAN.** Wow.

**HOWIE.** *Okay.*

**SOFIA.** Eva –

**EVA.** I also wanted to say sorry, Sofia – I left you hanging, earlier, but I *agree with you.* I feel like – that picture's really mean.

**HOWIE.** Well – *I...feel...*like it's really *nice*, so.

*(Pause.)*

And she liked it too. Her was *just* laughing at it.

**SOFIA.** Oh, I –

**EVA**. You were laughing at the Piss Chart?

(*Pause.*)

When?

**SOFIA**. Well, when you were in the bathroom, I realized that – it *is* funny, actually.

**EVA**. Because I thought...

**SOFIA**. To some people, it's funny. And to others it's less funny.

(*Pause.*)

And that's just – different feelings about this thing. And that's okay. Yeah?

**EVA**. (*Looking at* **SOFIA**, *not laughing.*) Oh. Okay.

(*Pause.*)

**SOFIA**. How about...next picture!

(*She holds up a picture of a woman crying.*)

So – what do you think is happening here?

**HOWIE**. (*Studying the picture.*) She's happy.

**SOFIA**. Is she, though? Really look at it, Howie. What expression is this woman making?

**HOWIE**. Ah...it looks like she's making...

**EVA**. Sorry, can we take a break?

**SOFIA**. Just – quickly, before that –

(*Back to* **HOWIE**.)

You were saying – it looks like she's making...

**EVA**. I said *I want to take a break*.

**SOFIA**. Ah...okay. Let's just – let's take a break, but just – Howie. Remember what you were saying, okay? And then – we can regroup after lunch.

**JORDAN**. Great – I'm actually super horn right now.

**HOWIE**. Same with me! Sofia? Want to eat lunch with me? Or – no, duh. Marcus.

**EVA**. Marcus?

**SOFIA**. That's my boyfriend.

**EVA**. I didn't know you had a boyfriend, Sofia.

> *(Matter-of-fact.)*

Hot name.

**HOWIE**. Eva? Want to watch me eat somewhere?

**EVA**. I need to talk to Sofia for a second.

**HOWIE**. Okay. Tooth.

> *(Proud.)*

Or, watch this, Sofia – "I *feel* like a tooth." Eh?

> *(He exits.)*

> (**EVA** *looks at* **SOFIA**.)

**SOFIA**. Is everything okay?

**EVA**. It's fine, I just –

> *(Pause.)*

Why did you laugh at their joke?

**SOFIA**. Look, I wasn't laughing *at* the joke. I mean – sure, I laughed at the joke, but I didn't think the joke was *funny*. I just – I need things to start moving forward. Not just for the sake of my job – for *your* sake, too.

**EVA**. You laughed at that horrible picture – for my sake?

**SOFIA**. Well – you saw what happened after I did that, right? They started participating! Jordan used the word "happy." We *finally* made *real progress* today! I'm telling you – in reality, I felt *nothing* about that joke.

**EVA**. Okay. Yes – okay, fine.

**SOFIA**. Also I asked Jon about the muggings again this morning, and he said he's on top of it. I promise you – I have your back.

**EVA**. Okay. Okay.

> *(Pause.)*

Do you ever wish that you knew yourself totally independent from everyone and everything that's ever touched you? Like, free of all context?

> *(Pause.)*

**EVA**. I had this picture of a mermaid in my room when I was little, and she always looked so happy. I mean, how cool is it to breathe underwater? And I used to think I was maybe kind of *like* her, in some way.

**SOFIA**. Sorry – one second. Howie e-mailed to say he's "meeting up with Marcus" – let me just...

**EVA**. *(Pause as* **SOFIA** *checks her phone.)* Anyways, one day this kid brought a Piss Chart into school and showed it to me during recess...and I went home feeling so sick to my stomach. And I looked up at the mermaid and I realized, like – duh – I could never be her! Because she *definitely* didn't know what a Piss Chart was, and I did. And I couldn't unlearn it.

**SOFIA**. *(She sends a response, looks up and focuses on* **EVA**.*)* Yes. A mermaid. Maybe one day you *will* be a mermaid.

*(She smiles.)*

Now let's go get some lunch!

## Scene Four

(**SOFIA** *is setting up a board and some papers
in the conference room. She's wearing a dress.
She checks her voice messages.*)

**SOFIA'S MOTHER.** Hi, dear. I wanted to try you again. It's
been three weeks now, and – well. Your father said he's
spoken to you a few times. And he said people are still
being a little tricky, at work. So I wanted to make sure
you're okay.

(*Pause.*)

He also told me that he told *you* about, ah...just to be
clear – I *don't* want you to pick sides! But I *did* want
to remind you that there are always *two*. So just *trust*
me that – yes, I did storm into his poker night and
I screamed so loudly that I shattered all the mirrors in
the house, but – I had my reasons. And so if you're not
calling me back because – if you think that I'm – if you
think I'm...what am I saying?

(*Trying to clear her head.*)

I'm just saying that it's still me over here. Your mother
who loves you, and who worries about you. Your mother
who cooks you Cheer-Me-Up burgers, who stole your
bike back from Micky, and who once made a cardboard
house with you that was so tall it hit the ceiling fan.

(*Pause. Affectionately.*)

So you call me back. Or I'll send a SWAT team after
you. I love you, my little spider. Bye bye.

(**SOFIA** *looks at her phone.* **JON** *enters.*)

**JON.** You look nice today! I hear you went out to dinner
with Jordan and Howie?

**SOFIA.** Yes! Jordan showed me how to order my big dog no
friends in French. And yesterday, Howie identified *five*
feelings for me. I mean, four of them were "hunger,"
but still.

**JON**. Yeah, I can see how much they've grown. It's all just – very...

*(He tries to find the right words.)*

Daddy says, "Good!"

*(He smiles.)*

So I guess you're ready to sign that paper?

**SOFIA**. Actually – not quite yet. Like, Jordan seems to *like* empathy now, which is great – but –

**JON**. But *what*, Sofia?

*(Exasperated.)*

Why are you always framing things in the negative? Think about where these guys *started*, and look at how far they've come!

**SOFIA**. But I think they may still think empathy's a bird. The other day at lunch they made a whole fuss over eating chicken...

**JON**. Who *cares*? *You* of all people should know that you can't blame someone for what they *feel*. If Jordan and Howie feel that empathy is a type of bird...if they feel it's a bird with sort-of...

*(He pictures a bird.)*

With strong, furry wings and big, detachable legs, then that's just not that big a deal. And if you're asking them to accommodate other people's feelings, I think it's only fair that you accommodate theirs as well. I guess here's what I'm getting at. I told head office this would be done by now, it *seems* done to me, and yet you keep finding ways to move the goalposts.

**SOFIA**. I'm not sure that's true.

**JON**. No? You think the two of us are getting somewhere? Or are *you* my cousin Rick, and *I'm* Auntie Eleanor, and we have these long and fruitful talks with one another but then at the end of the day, the *same* number of animals still end up inside the radiator with a note that says, "And once again, here be murdered babes"?

*(Pause.)*

**JON.** Some people are just...better at handling all different kinds of people. And if you're actually *as far* from finishing this job as you seem to think you are – then maybe you're just the wrong person to be handling these guys. You know? Maybe it would benefit *everyone* to bring someone else in instead.

**SOFIA.** But – no!

**JON.** It's not a *personal* thing! You're *objectively* really great, okay, but these guys are *tricky*, and it might just be better for them to –

**SOFIA.** Look. Let's set a goal of one more week. Okay?

>        *(**JON** eyes **SOFIA**.)*

I promise that I can get them to where they need to be. And I think you're exactly right – I should be taking their feelings into account. You're usually right about these things.

**JON.** Thanks. Do you like my arms?

**SOFIA.** Yes, I do.

**JON.** Well...you're good company for *me*, so – one more week.

**SOFIA.** Thanks. And – sorry, Jon, but I spoke to Eva and she still seems really nervous about those muggings.

**JON.** I *also* noticed that she was norvis about it –

**SOFIA.** *Nervous* about it –

**JON.** Right, sorry – nor...

>        *(He positions his mouth to get it right.)*

Nuer...veous about it...

**SOFIA.** So I'm wondering if you started that investigation yet?

**JON.** Yes! Of course I did. I said I would. Do you not trust me or something?

>        *(Hanging his head.)*

Guess my good-guy persona has a longer way to go than I thought.

**SOFIA.** No – I *trust* you. I just –

**JON.** Great, so let's bring this thing home together! Okay? Because as I like to say...

*(He thinks.)*

A window is nothing but a square that they cut out and they put glass in it. Okay? That's for damn sure.

*(He burrows into her, gives her a quick hug, and begins to exit. An* **OLD MAN** *enters.)*

Hey, buddy.

*(To* **SOFIA**.*)* Is this Marcus?

**SOFIA.** What? No, it's...

**JON.** I'll give you two some privacy.

*(***SOFIA** *looks at the* **OLD MAN**. *He stares back at her.)*

**OLD MAN.** I'm here to blow up this office.

**SOFIA.** You're here to –

**OLD MAN.** I don't mean to interrupt you, but I want to tell you a story first. Sit down!

*(He pauses.)*

When I was five years old, in kindergarten, our class would go out to the playground for recess. And I always dreaded the free period because, well, I had one friend, Joseph, who lived on my block, but he had a much easier time...*ingratiating* himself with the rest of the class, and so that meant I was usually alone during recess while everyone else played games.

*(Pause.)*

Anyways, one day I worked up the courage to just jump into the game and start running around! When all of a sudden a boy in my class, Sam, walked up to me, and told me that I couldn't play, because I was running in the wrong direction and I was messing up the game.

*(Pause.)*

**OLD MAN**. So I turned to my friend Joseph, because I knew he would vouch for me. And Sam and the other kids turned to Joseph too. And Joseph looked up, and he locked eyes with me, then he turned away.

*(He shudders.)*

So I walked off the playground and I started to cry. And this teacher from the other class came over to me, and she asked me *why* I was crying. And I wanted to explain it to her, but the place that my tears were coming from – it felt so complex that I didn't even know where to *begin*. Was I crying because I wasn't invited to play the game? Or because I had run the wrong direction? Or was it Sam, or Joseph, you know – all of my feelings were moving around so quickly inside of me that I couldn't get my finger onto any single one of them to keep it still and talk about it.

*(Pause.)*

So the teacher went over to Joseph to find out what happened. And as she walked away, I decided the most painless way to deal with all of these feelings was to push them outwards. I decided what I was feeling was anger, some complicated kind of *anger*, and I felt this incredible urge to express that anger onto everyone around me.

*(Pause.)*

Anyways, just as I was becoming increasingly trapped inside of my rage spiral, the teacher came back to me with all of the facts. And she knelt down to look at me, and she said, "So. You feel left out, huh?"

When she said that – it pulled me right out of that hole and placed me down on earth, beside her. Because suddenly, what I was feeling was very precise. And so – it still hurt, but it was one single thing, and it had a name. I didn't feel some complicated kind of anger. I felt *left out*.

**SOFIA**. Do I...know you?

**OLD MAN**. I only realized the comfort in that clarity later, when I no longer had it. Because of course, soon after that, I learned that crying is actually shorthand for being really, really weak, and so I stopped crying. And the good news is – not crying made me really strong, according to a really specific set of standards. And Sam started inviting me to play during recess. The bad news is that by never crying, teachers stopped approaching me to find out what was wrong, and I never learned about any new feelings. So now the only feelings I know are: being left out, being angry, being hungry and...there's one more, I think...

(*He shakes it off.*)

Anyways, you've made me feel *left out*, I think, or pretty close to it – some complicated kind of being left out, so... I went and got these bombs...from my kitchen...

(*He takes some cans out of his walker.*)

And now I'm going to blow up your office. I'm going to –

(**SOFIA** *sharply inhales. He starts pressing the cans.*)

Where are the buttons on these things? Where are –

**SOFIA**. That's...

(*She looks.*)

Dog food.

**OLD MAN**. What?

(*The tension has left the room.*)

**SOFIA**. You're holding dog food.

**OLD MAN**. Oh. So I am, yes. Shoot – that was a little silly of me.

(*He shakes his head.*)

I *knew* I should have brought my lucky egg with me, to pull this off.

**SOFIA**. Your lucky...wait a second...are you –

*(**EVA** enters.)*

**EVA.** *Rafalgore!*

*(Going over to **RAFALGORE**.)*

Rafalgore, what are you doing here? I'm sorry, Sofia, I – *(Angrily whispering to **RAFALGORE**.)* I thought I was very clear the last time we spoke. I don't want to see you anymore.

**OLD MAN.** You're...

*(He turns to **SOFIA**.)*

Who are you?

**SOFIA.** I'm Sofia.

**EVA.** You're looking for me. *I'm* Eva.

**OLD MAN.** Oh, right. I have a story to tell you.

*(He takes a breath.)*

I was on the playground –

**EVA.** You're not supposed to be here.

**OLD MAN.** The bottom line is that I was going to come in here and shoot up your office, but the gun was too heavy for me. So I brought these small bombs instead.

*(He pushes the cans again.)*

Where the *heck* are the buttons –

**SOFIA.** It's dog food.

**EVA.** Rafalgore. Those aren't bombs.

**OLD MAN.** No? Oh – darn! I'm feeling a really complicated kind of hunger right now!

*(He slaps his knee angrily, then looks down at his knee.)*

Uh oh, little Mr. Knee Cap – where the heck did you go, my best friend?

**EVA.** You have to leave.

**OLD MAN.** I used to take baseball bats and beat people's faces into the sidewalk for fun.

**EVA.** You already told me that.

**OLD MAN**. I once chugged gasoline to look tough and now the inside of my body looks like a bunch of Legos.

**EVA**. I *know*, and I'm serious, you've got to –

**OLD MAN**. *Fine.* I'll *go.*

*(She begins to escort him out of the office.)*

If I were forty years younger, I'd find a way to really hurt you. But I'm not ninety anymore.

*(**EVA** and **OLD MAN** exit. **HOWIE** and **JORDAN** enter.)*

**HOWIE**. Hey, Sofia. What's wrong?

**SOFIA**. How can you tell something's wrong?

**HOWIE**. Because you look – the face you taught us before.

*(He makes a scared face.)*

**JORDAN**. Yeah, you look scared right now.

**SOFIA**. I – *am* scared. Yes! Because someone just tried to blow up the office. And I'm so glad that you –

**HOWIE**. *What?* Who?

**SOFIA**. No – it's fine now. It was just Eva's ex-boyfriend.

**HOWIE**. Ugh.

**JORDAN**. Of course.

**SOFIA**. No, no – it's okay. Let's go back to –

**JORDAN**. *(He looks at her and thinks.)* You must feel *scared* right now.

**SOFIA**. I...right. You just said that. And I'm glad you can see it, because –

**HOWIE**. I'm sorry in quotes to interrupt you, but if you just said, "Eva's *ex*-boyfriend"...does that mean Eva's single?

**SOFIA**. Ah...well, I'm not sure, Howie –

**HOWIE**. Because I would – watch this, Sofia –

*(He chooses his words carefully.)*

I would *be curious* to see how she would feel about giving me a blowjob without reciprocation.

**JORDAN.** Oh, yeah. I feel that I *love* blowjobs without reciprocation.

**HOWIE.** I *also* feel that I love blowjobs without reciprocation!

**JORDAN.** I also feel that *I* love –

(**EVA** *re-enters, shaking her head.*)

**EVA.** Jeez. Rafalgore and his eggs! Sorry about that, Sofia.

**HOWIE.** I hear you're newly single?

**JORDAN.** More subtly, actually, we were wondering if you had a boyfriend...

**SOFIA.** Guys?

**HOWIE.** Sofia, if you don't mind...

(*There's incoherent screaming from offstage.*)

**SOFIA.** What's going on?

(*Everyone goes to the window, to look down below at the parking lot.*)

**EVA.** Oh.

(*Explaining.*)

Right as we were breaking up, Rafalgore realized that if he removes his leg from his hip, he can swing it around like a baseball bat.

**HOWIE.** I'm going out there.

**JORDAN.** I'm going too.

**HOWIE.** (*Valiantly, to* **EVA** *and* **SOFIA.**) We're going to protect you.

**JORDAN.** I'm a poet.

**EVA.** I don't think you have to –

(**HOWIE** *runs offstage.* **JORDAN** *follows him.* **SOFIA** *and* **EVA** *watch from inside.*)

Yeah, see – he's already asleep. Aw. Although when he wakes up he's going to say some shocking stuff.

**SOFIA.** (*Turning to* **EVA.**) Eva – while we have a second together...

**EVA.** Yes. I know. I scream-cried on the phone for an hour and a half the other day. I didn't realize who I was talking to. *I* definitely wasn't answering phones when *I* was a little baby...

**SOFIA.** No, no. It's just – you were right before...it might be a good idea for you to pretend that you're dating someone.

**EVA.** Oh. Why?

**SOFIA.** Because – well, you know these guys. They're so easily distracted. But I think they're *right* on the brink of really understanding empathy!

**EVA.** So you want me to...pretend I have a boyfriend. But isn't that going back on what you said before? Because – you told me to break up with Rafalgore, remember –

**SOFIA.** I know, yeah, but – I actually don't *mind* being with Marcus, you know, we get lunch together, and go to different ponds – and so... I think we can acknowledge *their* feelings, or, more specifically, their *horn*, and look at how *strong* their horn is, and say, "Okay. They need to work on that. But in the meantime, since it's not that big a deal to shift my behavior around just a *tiny* bit, maybe I should..."

**EVA.** Maybe I *should*...

(**SOFIA** *sees the men re-entering the office.*)

**SOFIA.** Look. We're up against a little bit of a clock, okay? So I think it's worth...being a little strategic here.

(**JORDAN** *and* **HOWIE** *enter the conference room.*)

**JORDAN.** Wow.

**HOWIE.** He *really* knows how to put together an upsetting sentence.

**JORDAN.** It never even *occurred* to me that you could use a towel that way.

**HOWIE.** Eva –

**SOFIA.** Thank you for protecting me, m'sir and m'sir. Let's jump right into today's exercise.

*(Going over to the board.)*

SOFIA. We're going to continue working on compassionate communication today.

*(She smiles.)*

So someone will describe a situation that elicits feelings in them. And then I want all of us to form sentences that follow this formula:

*(Pointing to the formula on the board.)*

"You feel blank because blank, is that right?" And then Person One will say, "Yes, that's right, I feel blank because blank," or, "No, that's not right, I do not feel blank because blank." Sound good? Who wants to start?

*(Pause. She looks around.)*

EVA. I can...

*(HOWIE's hand shoots up.)*

HOWIE. Sofia? I can start.

SOFIA. Great. Go ahead.

HOWIE. So this morning, I stood in front of my mother's grave site for like a half an hour, and I thought about how she was murdered – or, I guess not *murdered*, but, stabbed in the body until she died.

SOFIA. Okay. Thanks for sharing that with us. Who wants to respond to Howie?

EVA. *(Looking at the board.)* You feel *sad* because your mother was murdered, is that right?

SOFIA. Great! So, if that resonates –

HOWIE. *(Steamrolling her.)* No, that's not right, I do *not* feel sad because my mother was murdered.

SOFIA. Okay. Are you sure?

HOWIE. Yeah.

SOFIA. But – Howie. Have you ever been able to *really explore* how you *actually feel* about your mother's murder? Like – were you ever given permission to cry about it?

**HOWIE.** To *what* about it?

**SOFIA.** Cry.

(**HOWIE** *looks around.*)

**HOWIE.** Ah – I'm trying to understand what you're saying...

**JORDAN.** (*Gently and softly, to* **HOWIE.**) Howie, crying is when the top of a hose is connected to another hose, and so you can't figure out where the top one starts.

**SOFIA.** When – no. What I'm saying is – maybe you were taught that crying is a weakness. But it's not. It's a strength. And I want to give you permission to access your feelings.

**HOWIE.** Thank you, Sofia – but I really don't feel sad about my mother's murder. She died when I was *ten,* and the most I feel about it is...

**EVA.** Maybe you feel *powerless* because your mother was murdered.

**HOWIE.** *No,* I don't! I don't feel sad, and I don't feel powerless!

(*He throws a chair.*)

**SOFIA.** Now hold on a second –

**JORDAN.** Let me just – Howie!

(*Turning to* **HOWIE.**)

Maybe you feel...*nothing* about your mother's murder?

**HOWIE.** Maybe I feel...maybe I feel...

**JORDAN.** Maybe you feel *nothing.* Or, said differently – "You feel *nothing* because your mother was murdered. Is that right?"

**HOWIE.** I feel...oh my God. Of course.

(*He thinks, then gasps.*)

So many years replaying my mother's murder, and how I held her in my arms as she gasped for air and told me that she never really loved me, and I never understood how I felt about it. And now I know.

(*He takes a breath.*)

**HOWIE.** Yes. That's right. I feel *nothing* because my mother was murdered.

> *(He is breathless.)*

Oh, wow. I feel *so seen.* Thank you, Sofia.

**SOFIA.** You're...welcome.

> *(Pause.)*

**JORDAN.** I'd like to go.

**SOFIA.** Okay – great. Go ahead.

**JORDAN.** Well, so – yesterday, I asked a girl – I mean a woman – I mean an old woman – out on a date. I was sort of – ah – the word we learned the other day – vulner-ah-blay. And I guess – well, she said *no* to me, which is obviously her right, because keepee beepeep, but, yeah – she said no...and then all of these people around her – started laughing at me. And they were just laughing and laughing, as this enormous group and – so – yeah.

**SOFIA.** Wow. Okay – thanks. So who wants to go first?

**HOWIE.** I can.

> *(Looking at the board.)*

Jordan.

> *(Considering the sentence structure on the board.)*

You feel like – like, you were putting yourself out there, right, and she laughed at you for it, and so you were like – like – you, like – like like like –

**SOFIA.** Embarrassed?

**HOWIE.** Right – you feel *embarrassed* because you put yourself out there and you were laughed at for it, is that right?

**JORDAN.** Oh, I don't...

**SOFIA.** So – really think about that. Say it again.

**HOWIE.** You feel *embarrassed* because you *put yourself out there* and *you were laughed at for it*, is that right?

**SOFIA.** Jordan?

**JORDAN.** Well, I guess just a little.

**SOFIA.** Say it back as –

**JORDAN.** Yes, that's right – I feel embarrassed because I put myself out there and I was laughed at for it.

**SOFIA.** *Good.* Good job, guys.

> *(She turns to* **EVA.***)*

Eva?

**EVA.** You feel ashamed because you were made to feel small, is that right?

**JORDAN.** Yes, that's right. I feel ashamed because I was made to feel small.

**SOFIA.** Great, Eva – *great*, Jordan.

**HOWIE.** You feel –

*(To* **SOFIA.***)* When you don't feel big?

**SOFIA.** Small.

**HOWIE.** You feel *small* because you were dismissed.

**JORDAN.** Yes. I feel small...

> *(He begins to tear up.)*

Yes, I feel small because – I was dismissed.

> *(Processing this.)*

I feel *small* because...

> *(***JORDAN*** bursts into tears; he continues to cry throughout this next exchange.)*

Oh God! Yes, yes – that's right! She made me feel small! Oh no – now I'm hose on top of a hose so you can't see where the top one starts!

**SOFIA.** It's okay. That's *good*.

**JORDAN.** I was just using my normal line of saying, "Do you want to see a show-y?"

**SOFIA.** "Do you want to –" What's a show-y?

**JORDAN.** A show-y!

**HOWIE.** It's what you leave sort of open!

**JORDAN.** And she told me to stop talking to her...when I just wanted to do a little show-y...

**SOFIA.** So you can also *do* a show-y...

**JORDAN.** And the security guards started asking if I even had a *ticket* to this stupid charity dinner...and they began forcing me off the stage...

**SOFIA.** Off the – stage...

**JORDAN.** I bet she didn't even deserve that award! I don't even know what an oncologist *is*!

**HOWIE.** No one does!

**JORDAN.** *(Scream-crying.)* She was just so freaking hot –

**HOWIE.** I *understand*, Jordan –

**JORDAN.** *(Overlapping.)* And I just wanted to do a big show-y –

**HOWIE & JORDAN.** All over her tits!

**HOWIE.** Of course you did!

**JORDAN.** *(Overlapping.)* I'm a poet!

**HOWIE.** You're a poet!

**JORDAN.** Life is an oblong! *Nice guys always finish last!*

**HOWIE.** *(Like a monster.) We always finish last!*

> (**JORDAN** *lets out a scream-sob.*)

Do you see, Sofia? We're doing it! We're really doing it.

> (*A bird flies across the stage.*)

Oh wow – look!

> (*In awe.*)

*Empathy.*

> (*The men stare at the bird.* **SOFIA** *watches them warily.*)

**JORDAN.** *(Wiping his tears away.)* Wow.

> (*Laughing.*)

We solved it. We solved empathy.

**HOWIE & JORDAN.** We. Solved. Empathy!

*(Pause.)*

**EVA.** I want to go.

**SOFIA.** Okay, great.

**JORDAN.** I'm shaking.

**SOFIA.** Okay, go ahead Eva.

**EVA.** The first time I got mugged in this office was two years ago.

**SOFIA.** Ah – hm. Eva? Let's just –

**EVA.** After it happened... The world was so normal when it was over. It was so exactly the same that the mugging started to feel like like this strange blip, to the point where I actually started wondering whether I had made the whole thing up, or drastically mis-remembered it or something. I thought, "Huh. That *felt* like such a big thing to *me*, but clearly it was *not* actually a big thing." Then it started happening more and more. This morning, I was mugged on my way into the kitchen to get some coffee. The person came up behind me and hit me across the side of my head...and I couldn't really feel it, but I touched my ear, and I noticed I was bleeding.

*(Pause.)*

Anyways, suddenly I was on the floor of the kitchen in a ball, and I wasn't being mugged anymore. So I went back to my desk without getting my coffee – and the world was still...the same.

*(Long pause. Everyone looks at her.)*

Is someone going to respond?

**SOFIA.** Yes. We're *all* going to respond, right guys? Can we respond to Eva, using the sentence structure?

**JORDAN.** Eva. You feel *tired* because *you didn't get your coffee*, is that right?

**EVA.** Yes, I guess so. But that's not really –

**SOFIA.** And so – we'll keep finding – but in the meantime, say the full sentence back to him: "Yes, that's right – I feel tired because..."

**EVA**. Yes, that's right – I feel tired because I didn't get my coffee.

**JORDAN**. You feel mugged because you got mugged.

**SOFIA**. Okay, let's – anyone else? Howie?

**HOWIE**. *(Looking at the list.)* You feel *content* because you got mugged...you feel *improbablay* because you got mugged...you feel *thrilled, inquisitive* and *hopeful* because you got mugged.

**EVA**. No. I *don't*. That is *so wrong*.

**HOWIE**. Whoa. Sorry.

**SOFIA**. Now – hold on, guys. Howie – Eva is sharing something sensitive with you – and Eva, Howie was patient with you when you assumed he felt sad about his mother's murder. It's really important that we stay *respectful* of one another.

*(Gently, to* **HOWIE** *and* **JORDAN**.*)* Maybe you guys want to try some words from the bottom of the list?

**JORDAN**. Where?

*(Looking at the page down.)*

You feel distressed because you got mugged?

**EVA**. Yes! Yes, that's right, I feel distressed because I got mugged.

**SOFIA**. Good, Eva! Good, Jordan!

**HOWIE**. Where did you find that word? What does that mean?

**JORDAN**. Down under the "difficult slash unpleasant feelings" part.

*(***HOWIE** *looks down.)*

**HOWIE**. These are all real words?

*(Reading from the list.)*

You feel *lost* because you got mugged, is that right?

**EVA**. Yes, that's right – I feel lost because I got mugged.

**HOWIE**. You feel in despair and disappointed because you got mugged, is that right? You feel alarmed, anxious, panic, doubtful –

**JORDAN.** You feel wary, afflicted, heartbroken, and wronged because you got mugged, is that right?

**EVA.** Yes! That's right.

**JORDAN.** You feel *weak* because you got mugged.

**EVA.** I guess – that's also right, in a way...

**HOWIE.** You feel *inferior* because you got mugged.

**SOFIA.** As a question.

> (**HOWIE** *speaks the next sentence fully like it's a command, but makes a question-mark up-sound after it.*)

**HOWIE.** You feel *inferior* because *you got mugged.* Eh?

**EVA.** I mean – I guess I...

**SOFIA.** Using the formula?

**EVA.** I don't – I'm having some trouble...

**JORDAN.** I can say it too, if that helps.

> (**JORDAN** *moves closer to* **EVA.**)

You must feel very inferior because you got mugged. Very inferior, and very humiliated. Is that right?

**EVA.** *(Emotional.)* Yes. That's right.

**HOWIE.** This must be so difficult slash unpleasant.

**EVA.** It is. It really, really is.

> (*She starts to cry.* **HOWIE** *moves closer to her.*)

**HOWIE.** Well, I'm glad that we're connecting, even though needless to say I wish it were under better circumstances...

> (*He moves in for a kiss.*)

**EVA.** *(Snapping out of it.)* Wait – no.

**SOFIA.** Okay – hold on...

**JORDAN.** If I can make this exchange more subtle...

> (**HOWIE** *and* **JORDAN** *move closer to* **EVA.** *She screams.*)

**EVA.** I don't want to kiss you. I don't want to kiss either of you.

**SOFIA.** Because aren't you dating someone, Eva? Aren't you dating... Marcus?

**EVA.** No, I'm *not*. I don't want to kiss either of you because you guys make me feel unsafe.

**HOWIE.** *What?*

**JORDAN.** Wow.

**EVA.** Sofia?

**SOFIA.** Well...

> *(Pause as* **SOFIA** *looks at the men, and then turns to* **EVA.***)*

I'm sure they don't *mean* to make you feel unsafe.

**EVA.** *(Frantically and angrily.)* Well, they *do,* Sofia – what do you *mean* they don't mean to? I'm telling you that they *do*!

**SOFIA.** Hey! I'm trying to *juggle* a lot of people right now, and empathize with everyone...

**EVA.** You're not *empathizing* with me!

**SOFIA.** I *am* empathizing with you! I *understand*, okay, you feel *unsafe*, and *norvis*, and it makes me sick to my *stomach*. But –

**EVA.** Nervous.

**SOFIA.** What did I say?

**EVA.** You said "norvis."

**SOFIA.** Okay, but –

**EVA.** I want to be left alone.

**SOFIA.** Fine. Why don't we just – take a breather. Eva, let's get some lunch –

**EVA.** *(A little unhinged.)* I said I want to be left alone! I want to be left alone! *I want to be left alone!*

> *(***EVA** *exits. Pause.)*

**HOWIE.** Jeez.

**JORDAN.** Yeah.

**HOWIE.** So much for professionalism.

## Scene Five

**SOFIA'S MOTHER**. Hi, my little spider.

*(Pause.)*

I still haven't heard from you. And I don't know. I thought maybe you were just – not doing well or something, I was *worried* you weren't doing well, but – I hear you're doing well. I hear from *your father* that you're doing well. And I'm glad to hear it. I just... I'm not doing well.

*(Pause.)*

And I don't know. Your father's taken so much of my world from me. And now I'm standing here like – are you gone too?

*(Pause.)*

Whatever's happening, I feel like I'm bothering you. So I'm going to leave you alone. I love you. Okay – bye.

> (**SOFIA** *is in the conference room, setting up.* **JON**, **HOWIE**, *and* **JORDAN** *enter together, happily.*)

**JON**. Congratulations!

The guys told me over lunch that they solved empathy.

**SOFIA**. That they...

**JON**. And so I thought we could celebrate as soon as you sign that paper!

**SOFIA**. Actually – we're not done quite yet. We have more exercises to go through.

**HOWIE**. Is this a joke?

**SOFIA**. It's *great* that you guys have gotten in touch with empathy. And now we have to apply that empathy to your work calls.

**HOWIE**. But –

**JON**. *Sofia.*

**SOFIA.** *(To* **JON.***)* If you'd like to watch for a second, maybe you'll see what I mean.

*(Checking her watch.)*

Where's Eva?

**JORDAN.** She's in the bathroom.

**SOFIA.** Fine, then – let's just start. The phone call we listened to week one, with Donna. Here's a recap of her situation, on these sheets...

*(***SOFIA*** begins to hand out sheets of paper to everyone.)*

So Donna's husband was sick, right, he was back in the hospital, and Donna owed money that she didn't have. So using the sentence structure, tell me how Donna must be feeling. Howie.

**HOWIE.** I don't know Donna. She's not even here.

**SOFIA.** Pretend I'm Donna.

**HOWIE.** "You feel like an idiot, Donna, because you spent money that you didn't have, is that right?"

**SOFIA.** Howie...try again please, without the judgment.

**HOWIE.** Okay. Without the judgment, I could say...

*(Looking directly at* **SOFIA.***)*

Pay the money.

**SOFIA.** Using the sentence structure.

**HOWIE.** You feel scared because if you don't pay the money, I'm going to hurt you, is that right?

*(***SOFIA*** inhales sharply and looks directly at him.)*

**SOFIA.** No, that's not right. Try again. And this time –

*(***HOWIE*** stands up.)*

What are you doing?

**HOWIE.** I'm looking for my baseball bat.

**SOFIA.** What do you need your baseball bat for? You're talking to someone on the phone.

**HOWIE.** No, I'm not – you're right in front of me.

**JORDAN.** Sofia, you're being really hard on us. I noticed that you weren't sad for me *at all* about the traumatic situation I went through with the pediatric oncologist who was getting a Lifetime Achievement Award for creating a new technology to save terminally ill children.

**SOFIA.** *Excuse* me?

**HOWIE.** Where the *hell's* my bat?

**SOFIA.** Let's remember compassionate communication, Howie...

**JORDAN.** You feel like your bat is behind the bookshelf because Jon put it behind the bookshelf, is that right?

(**HOWIE** *grabs his bat. He holds it up, angrily.*)

**JON.** Oh darn. Howie! I'm with you, all right? Just put the bat down. I'm with you.

(**HOWIE** *puts the bat down.* **SOFIA** *turns to* **JON.***)*

**SOFIA.** Thanks, Jon.

(*Smoothing out her dress.*)

Let's take a break.

**JON.** *(Disapprovingly.)* Take a *break*? Sofia...

**SOFIA.** "*Sofia*" what?

**JON.** I can't believe I didn't see it before. No *wonder* you haven't had success here! You're *provoking* my employees.

**SOFIA.** How am I *provoking* them?

**JON.** By telling them that other people's feelings should outweigh theirs! You're asking them to change their entire *worldview*!

(*Pause.*)

I have used so many different strategies with you. I've spoken your language, I've been the Auntie Eleanor to your Rick. But at some point, you know, I have to be the boss. I have to take care of my family.

*(He begins to sign the paper himself.)*

**SOFIA.** You can't just...sign it.

**JON.** I *did* just sign it. So I think we're done here.

**SOFIA.** Fine.

*(She starts to leave.)*

**HOWIE.** Hey – I heard you got fired. Want to talk about it over a drink?

**JORDAN.** Want to talk about it on top of a pond?

**SOFIA.** No, because – Marcus!

**HOWIE.** Marcus, right. Marcus is cheating on you.

**JORDAN.** We saw him in a grocery store last night, getting a blowjob without reciprocation from hundreds of women.

**SOFIA.** No you didn't.

**HOWIE.** And there was a catfish watching, just off to the side –

**SOFIA.** You didn't see that.

*(Turning to* **JON**.*)*

Jon?

*(Pause.)*

**JON.** *(Turning to* **HOWIE** *and* **JORDAN**.*)* Yeah – guys...

*(Pause. He sighs.)*

The Marcus thing. I saw it too. It's terrible, really – some men can be such pigs. Awful, awful.

*(He brightens.)*

So! How do you feel about blowjobs without reciprocation?

*(The men start to close in on her.)*

**JORDAN.** How do you feel about my poetry?

**HOWIE.** For me personally, I *love* blowjobs without reciprocation.

*(They all laugh.* **SOFIA** *tries to join in half-heartedly.)*

**HOWIE**. Why are you laughing?

**SOFIA**. Because it's a joke.

**HOWIE**. I don't think you get it.

**SOFIA**. Well all the same, maybe we can just –

> *(Pause.)*

You wouldn't want to make me feel – remember scared?

**JORDAN**. Lighten up.

**HOWIE**. I love blowjobs without reciprocation.

**JORDAN**. I love them too.

**JON**. I do too. I think *they're* what I love the best.

**SOFIA**. Get *away from me*.

> *(She picks up* **HOWIE***'s baseball bat.)*

**JORDAN**. Calm down.

**HOWIE**. You're acting crazy.

**JON**. C'mon, Sofia – meet us halfway.

**SOFIA**. Meet you halfway?

> *(Pause as she computes this.)*

I am meeting you *all the way*! You haven't moved *an inch.*

> *(Getting increasingly angry.)*

I listen to you, I cater to you, I call you on the phone...

**JON**. Call us on the phone?

**SOFIA**. Well – not *you*, but –

> *(She screams and smashes the bat onto the table.)*

## Scene Six

*(Bathroom stalls appear onstage. Someone is in one stall with the door closed, and* **JANIE** *sits in the other stall on the toilet with the door open, going through her purse. She's wearing her cardigan and holding her mug from the office.)*

*(***SOFIA*** bursts into the room.)*

**JANIE.** Hi.

*(Looking at her.)*

You must feel scared right now.

**SOFIA.** I do. I do feel scared.

**JANIE.** Do you want to sit down?

*(***SOFIA*** sits. ***JANIE*** smiles at her and then turns to the closed bathroom stall. ***EVA*** speaks from the stall.)*

**EVA.** What were you saying? I'm still listening.

**JANIE.** Oh... I was saying that – I agree with you. Nothing happens in a split second. One tiny moment after one tiny moment turns into a *big* moment. So it's hard to blame *anyone* in one of those tiny moments – because it's hard to even recognize it as a moment in the first place! And what does that do to you?

*(She thinks.)*

I think when no one's reacting to it, you assume it must be normal. You put it onto yourself – you figure if you're the *only* person clocking this little *thing* as being some sort of *problem*, then *you* must be wrong. *You* must be the problem. And you sit alone with that and it seeps into your pores, and it morphs into...well, *that* becomes self-loathing. And meanwhile, all those little moments keep piling on top of one another.

*(Pause.)*

And then all of a sudden you look up, and you're setting the office on fire.

(**EVA** *comes out of the stall dressed like a mermaid. She begins to wash her hands.*)

**JANIE.** And just to be really honest – I mean, at the end of the day, I *do* blame him. But more to the point, I'm mostly focused on not blaming myself.

**EVA.** Yes. That's a nice way of saying that.

**JANIE.** And I've decided that in the end, it's really not a *bad* thing to blame someone for wearing you down. Especially when you realize – they're only right because *they're* making up the rules.

**EVA.** *(She looks at* **JANIE**.*)* I understand – and Janie. I also know I let you down.

**SOFIA.** Eva.

**EVA.** *(She sees* **SOFIA**.*)* Oh – hi.

**SOFIA.** You look beautiful.

**EVA.** Thanks.

**JANIE.** Are you here to sync up with us?

**SOFIA.** No, I –

**JANIE.** *(Entering the stall.)* Wait, wait. Or – no, keep going. But talk louder so that I can pee.

(*She closes the stall and begins to pee.*)

**SOFIA.** I came here to be alone. I'm not even on my period.

**EVA.** That's okay. Janie never gets hers.

**JANIE.** It's true.

**SOFIA.** Then how...?

**EVA.** Well, she can still *bleed*.

**SOFIA.** What about you?

**EVA.** Yes. I'm bleeding.

**SOFIA.** Mermaids still get their periods?

(*Looking at her.*)

But where does it come from, when you have a tail?

**EVA.** No. I already told you.

**SOFIA.** You did?

**EVA.** Yes. Remember? I *told* you I was bleeding.

(**SOFIA** *looks at* **EVA.** **JANIE** *exits the stall. She's bleeding from her nose.*)

**SOFIA.** Careful – your – your nose is...

(*She goes over to* **JANIE** *and puts a paper towel under her nose. She then looks at* **EVA***, who is bleeding from her ear.*)

Oh God – your ear!

(*She runs over to* **EVA** *and starts trying to clean up the blood. There's a lot of it. The paper towels don't really help.*)

Why is it – it won't stop!

**JANIE.** No, it won't.

**EVA.** Oh – careful. Your hands.

**SOFIA.** My hands?

(*She looks down at her hands and sees that they're covered in blood.* **SOFIA** *turns to* **EVA***.*)

Eva.

**EVA.** I can't forgive you.

**SOFIA.** You can't?

**EVA.** I can't hear you! I've got blood in my ears.

**SOFIA.** Okay, but all the same. I should have –

**EVA.** I said I can't hear you, Sofia.

(*The lights change. The bathroom is gone.* **SOFIA** *is alone on stage, still covered in blood. She stands in silence. Then she picks up her phone and calls someone. Across the stage,* **SOFIA'S MOTHER** *walks over to a ringing phone.*)

**SOFIA'S MOTHER.** Hello?

**SOFIA.** Mama? Mama!

**SOFIA'S MOTHER.** *Sofia.*

(**SOFIA** *begins to cry.*)

**SOFIA.** I couldn't – I should have –

*(Pause.)*

I'm *sorry.*

*(**SOFIA***'s mother basks in her daughter's voice.)*

**SOFIA'S MOTHER.** My little spider.

**SOFIA.** How are you feeling?

## End of Play

Printed in the USA
CPSIA information can be obtained
at www.ICGtesting.com
LVHW020759200324
774984LV00004B/468

9 780573 707988